More fun by Adam Bestwick...

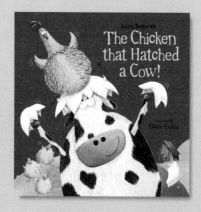

First published in Great Britain in 2017 by Fourth Wall Publishing
2 Riverview Business Park, Shore Wood Road,
Bromborough, Wirral CH62 3RQ

'When The Sky Was Too Low' ISBN: 978-1-910851-29-6

Printed in China.

fourth wall
publishing

When the Sky was too Low

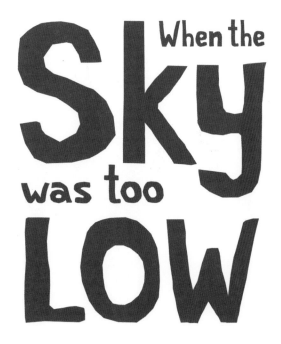

Written and illustrated by
Adam Bestwick

Based on a
Native American story
from the Snohomish tribe

Once upon a time,
many years ago, the sky
wasn't high like it is today—
it was annoyingly low.

The trees were unable to grow tall
so they curled into whatever
space they could find.
Birds couldn't fly so their wings became
small and they walked on the floor.

Other animals were very different too.
Giraffe's necks went sideways, kangaroos couldn't jump and
elephants, who had no space to grow, were as small as horses!

Not high!

Buildings were built low to the ground, and there were no rockets, no planes and no stairs up.
In fact, there was no up!

Clouds couldn't find their own place,
so they bunched together.
Kites got stuck and balls were lost within
the huge expanse of white fluffiness.
This made the children very sad.

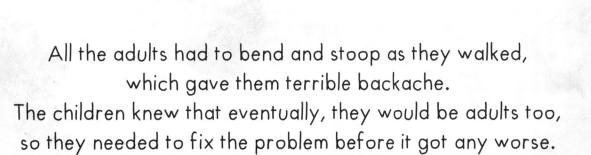

All the adults had to bend and stoop as they walked,
which gave them terrible backache.
The children knew that eventually, they would be adults too,
so they needed to fix the problem before it got any worse.

One day, a curious boy was looking for his ball.
He climbed on the neck of a giraffe and asked him to lift his head
into the clouds. They were both a little scared at first,
but as the giraffe's neck poked through, they found...

...EMPTY SPACE.

And lots of it!

Quickly, he climbed down
and ran off to tell the other children
about his amazing discovery!

The boy told them all about the empty space above the clouds.
They talked for hours, and eventually they made a plan
to try and lift the sky.

Wherever the children went,
they collected sticks.

The longest ones they could find.

They all came together, and using the sticks,
they pushed and poked and pushed again.
But the sticks weren't long enough
and the sky didn't budge.

The adults laughed
at them,
but the children
were determined
not to be beaten.

Another meeting was held, and after some careful thinking,
the children had an even better idea!
Using some string, they tied the sticks together to make...

THE MOST
ENORMOUS STICK
EVER SEEN!

It was
so big and so long,
that you couldn't see
the end of it!

The children all worked together
to raise the giant stick.
Some of them pushed and some of them pulled,
until slowly, the stick went higher
and the clouds began to rise!

A loud BOOM of thunder
told the children that the sky was
as high as it would go.
They all gave a huge cheer!

Finally, with the sky lifted,
clouds could move and find their own space.
Birds could fly joyfully and trees were free to grow
as tall as skyscrapers.

The giraffes lifted their heads high,
kangaroos jumped for joy...

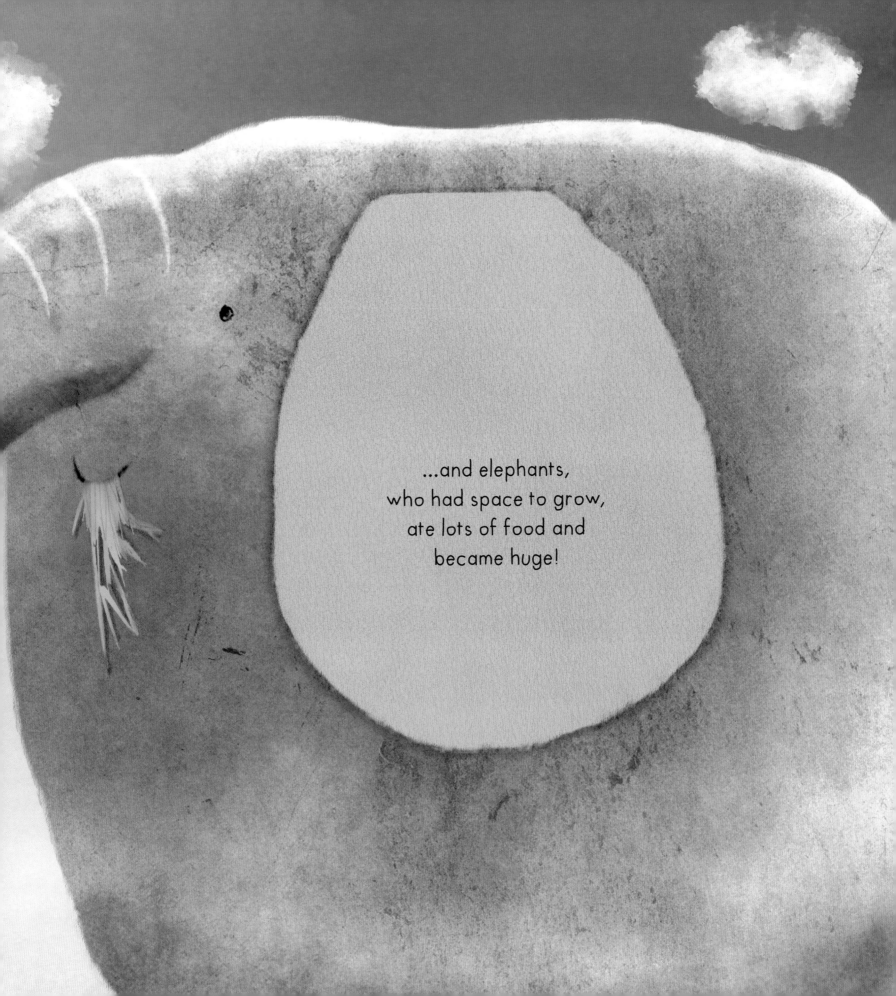

...and elephants,
who had space to grow,
ate lots of food and
became huge!

Mega high!

With so much space above them,
the people of the town no longer walked bent over.
They built super tall buildings that were higher than the trees,
and even planes so they could enjoy the sky.

Balls no longer got stuck in the clouds,
and the children could fly their kites
as high as they would go!

From then on, when it got dark,
the sky was filled with the most amazing
sparkling lights all over the sky!

Next time you go to bed,
look up and remember...

Every sparkly white light is a hole in the sky where the children poked their sticks through.